Disney

5 Minute Christmas Stories

Disney PRESS
Los Angeles • New York

Copyright © 2016 Disney Enterprises, Inc.

"Santa's Little Helper" by Kate Ritchey. Copyright © 2016 Disney
Enterprises, Inc.

"A Gift for WALL•E" by Tennant Redbank. Copyright © 2009 Disney
Enterprises, Inc. Based on characters from the movie *WALL•E*. Copyright
© 2008 Disney Enterprises, Inc./Pixar.

"Christmas in Never Land" by Megan Bryant. Copyright © 2016 Disney
Enterprises, Inc. Based on characters from the movie *Peter Pan*. Copyright
© 1953 Disney Enterprises, Inc.

"A Present for the Queen" by Tracey West. Copyright © 2016 Disney
Enterprises, Inc. Based on characters from the movie *Alice in Wonderland*.
Copyright © 1951 Disney Enterprises, Inc.

"Snow Puppies" adapted from the book *Snow Puppies* by Barbara Bazaldua,
published by Golden Books Publishing Company, Inc. Copyright © 1996.
Based on the characters from the movie *One Hundred and One Dalmatians*.
Copyright © 1961 Disney Enterprises, Inc. *One Hundred and One Dalmatians*
is based on the book *The Hundred and One Dalmatians* by Dodie Smith,
published by The Viking Press.

"Christmas in Monstropolis" by Gail Herman. Copyright © 2016 Disney
Enterprises, Inc. Based on characters from the movie *Monsters, Inc.*
Copyright © 2001 Disney Enterprises, Inc./Pixar.

"Merry Christmas, Winnie the Pooh" adapted by Megan Ilnitzki.
Copyright © 2016 Disney Enterprises, Inc. Based on the "Winnie the
Pooh" works by A. A. Milne and E. H. Shepard. All rights reserved.

"Aurora's Homemade Holiday" by Lisa Ann Marsoli. Copyright © 2014
Disney Enterprises, Inc. Based on characters from the movie *Sleeping
Beauty*. Copyright © 1959 Disney Enterprises, Inc.

"Christmas Traditions" by Kate Ritchey. Copyright © 2016 Disney
Enterprises, Inc. Based on characters from the movie *Lady and the Tramp*.
Copyright © 1955 Disney Enterprises, Inc.

"Mater Saves Christmas" adapted by Megan Ilnitzki. Based on the book
by Kiel Murray, copyright © 2012 Disney Enterprises, Inc. Based on
characters from the movie *Cars*. Copyright © 2006 Disney Enterprises,
Inc./Pixar. Disney/Pixar elements © Disney/Pixar, not including
underlying vehicles owned by third parties: Background is inspired by
Cadillac Ranch by Ant Farm (Lord, Michels and Marquez) © 1974; Hudson
Hornet is a trademark of Chrysler LLC; Chevrolet Impala is a trademark of
General Motors; Fiat is a trademark of Fiat S.p.A.; Porsche is a trademark

of Porsche; Volkswagen trademarks, design patents, and copyrights are
used with the approval of the owner, Volkswagen AG; Jeep® and the Jeep®
grille design are registered trademarks of Chrysler LLC; Sarge's rank
insignia design used with the approval of the U.S. Army; Ferrari elements
are trademarks of Ferrari S.p.A.; Mercury and Model T are registered
trademarks of Ford Motor Company.

"A Meowy Christmas" by Brittany Rubiano. Copyright © 2016 Disney
Enterprises, Inc. Based on characters from the movie *Pinocchio*. Copyright
© 1940 Disney Enterprises, Inc.

"A Perfect Party" by Lisa Ann Marsoli. Copyright © 2014 Disney
Enterprises, Inc. Based on characters from the movie *Cinderella*. Copyright
© 1950 Disney Enterprises, Inc.

All illustrations by the Disney Storybook Art Team

All rights reserved. Published by Disney Press, an imprint of Disney Book
Group. No part of this book may be reproduced or transmitted in any
form or by any means, electronic or mechanical, including photocopying,
recording, or by any information storage and retrieval system, without
written permission from the publisher.

For information address Disney Press, 1101 Flower Street, Glendale,
California 91201.

Printed in the United States of America

First Edition, September 2016

Library of Congress Control Number: 2015946852

1 3 5 7 9 10 8 6 4 2

ISBN 978-1-4847-2741-6

FAC-038091-16211

For more Disney Press fun, visit www.disneybooks.com

SUSTAINABLE FORESTRY INITIATIVE
Certified Sourcing
www.sfiprogram.org
SFI-00993
This Label Applies to Text Stock Only

Contents

Santa's Little Helper

It was Christmas Eve, and all was quiet. Mickey and Pluto were fast asleep when . . . *Achoo! Achoo! Achoo!*

A chorus of sneezes outside woke them. They ran to the window to see the commotion.

Mickey couldn't believe his eyes: Santa Claus was standing in his backyard! Attached to Santa's sleigh were nine reindeer with bright red noses. *That's funny,* Mickey thought to himself. *Isn't Rudolph supposed to be the only one with a red nose?*

Mickey ran outside in his pajamas. "Merry Christmas, Santa!" he said. "Is something wrong?"

"It's all this sneezing!" Santa said. "Dasher was sniffling when we left the North Pole, and now everyone but Rudolph has come down with a bad cold! We all need to get home to bed, but we still have four houses to visit."

The reindeer promptly let out another round of sneezes. They looked miserable! But what could Santa do? He couldn't leave his last four houses without Christmas presents!

"Gee, maybe Pluto and I can help," Mickey said. "We'd be happy to deliver the presents for you!"

"Oh, thank you, Mickey!" Santa said. He lifted a huge red sack out of his sleigh. "My gift sack is full of Christmas magic; it will help you make the deliveries."

Santa Claus handed Mickey a list of presents to deliver. Then he climbed back into his sleigh and the reindeer slowly lifted off into the sky, coughing and sneezing all the way.

Mickey pulled his sled from the garage and hauled it over to the giant sack of gifts. He expected the bag to be very heavy, but when he picked it up, it was as light as a feather!

"That must be the Christmas magic Santa mentioned," Mickey said. "Come on, Pluto, let's finish Santa's deliveries!"

Pluto grabbed the sled's rope in his mouth. He stepped
forward to pull it behind him, when suddenly . . .

Pluto, Mickey, and the sled rose into the air. They were flying!

"Whoa! More Christmas magic!" Mickey said, holding on tight
as the sled steered itself to their first stop.

In no time at all, the sled landed on Daisy's roof. Mickey and Pluto quickly hopped out.

"Hmmm, how do you think I get inside?" Mickey asked, lifting the Christmas sack over his shoulder. "Santa goes down the chimney. Should I try?"

Pluto nodded, and Mickey walked to the chimney. He leaned over and looked down. Before he knew it, he was sliding into Daisy's living room! He landed on the ground with a puff of chimney soot.

"This Christmas magic takes some getting used to," he said as he rubbed his sore backside.

Mickey looked over Santa's list and then took Daisy's gifts from the giant sack. He had just finished arranging them under the tree when he saw the treats Daisy had left for Santa.

"I'm sure she wouldn't mind if I ate them, since I'm filling in for Santa," Mickey said, happily munching on the cookies.

Mickey quickly filled Daisy's stocking and then looked up the chimney. Suddenly, *whoosh!* Mickey was whisked back to the roof! When he saw Pluto, Mickey realized he hadn't brought a cookie for his friend.

"I'm sorry, Pluto! I promise I'll get you a treat at the next house," he said.

The next delivery was for Goofy. Mickey had just leaned into the chimney when Pluto grabbed the back of the sack in his teeth. He didn't want to miss getting a treat at *this* house! The Christmas magic whisked them both down the chimney and into Goofy's living room.

"Pluto!" Mickey said. "I promised that I'd bring you a—oh, no look out!"

Spotting the plate of cookies Goofy had left for Santa, Pluto ran right toward it. But he accidentally brushed against Goofy's tree! It went crashing to the ground.

Mickey and Pluto fixed Goofy's tree as best they could, but it still drooped a little on one side.

Mickey checked his list and got his friend's presents out of Santa's sack. "Maybe he'll be so excited about his gifts that he won't even notice the tree," he said.

Mickey very carefully filled Goofy's stocking, and then he and Pluto went back up the chimney to their sled.

Mickey and Pluto had to hurry. They
had spent so long fixing Goofy's tree that
they were running out of time to deliver
the rest of Santa's gifts!

At Minnie's house, Mickey rushed down
the chimney, checking Santa's list on the
way. He pulled her gifts from Santa's sack,
placed them under the tree, and then
filled her stocking with goodies. On his
way back to the chimney, he grabbed two
cookies—one for him and one for Pluto.

When they landed on Donald's roof, Mickey got right to work: he dropped down the chimney, pulled out the list, and headed straight to the tree. He pulled Donald's presents from the sack: one, two, three . . .

"Uh-oh," Mickey said. "There are supposed to be four gifts, but there are only three left in the bag! Did I drop one?"

Mickey looked everywhere: by the chimney, under the table, behind the chair. . . . As he was crouching to look beneath the sofa, Mickey heard footsteps upstairs. Donald was awake!

Mickey grabbed Santa's sack and raced to the chimney.

"The stocking!" he cried. Mickey quickly filled his friend's stocking. He had just finished when one of Donald's feet appeared at the top of the stairs!

Luckily, Santa's Christmas magic was waiting. It whisked Mickey up the chimney seconds before Donald came downstairs.

"Whew!" Mickey said as he and Pluto flew home. "That was way too close!"

The next morning, the friends all met at Mickey's house for Christmas breakfast. It seemed everyone had a different story about Santa's visit the previous night!

"Santa must have been a little out of sorts last night," Daisy said to Goofy. "He left chimney soot all over my floor. He's never done anything like that before."

"I know what you mean," Goofy said. "I think Santa bumped into my tree; it looked a little lopsided this morning."

"He woke me up with all the noise he was making!" Donald exclaimed. "He's always been so quiet."

"I almost forgot!" Minnie said to Donald. "Santa left one of your presents at my house."

Suddenly, Mickey realized that he had left Santa's magic sack next to his tree. He looked around worriedly, but the sack was gone. In its place was a box with a tag that said *Love, Santa*.

Mickey unwrapped the box. Inside was a beautiful snow globe of Pluto and Mickey riding with Santa in his sleigh.

Mickey winked at Pluto. "No, Santa Claus definitely wasn't himself last night!" he said. "Merry Christmas, everybody!"

Disney · PIXAR

WALL·E

A Gift for WALL·E

WALL·E and EVE peeked over the top of a pile of garbage. The humans were acting strange. What were they up to now?

They saw two men stringing small colored lights along a rusty iron fence. Another set up a plastic statue of a fat, white-bearded man in a red suit, red hat, and black boots. Strangest of all, the Captain from the spaceship *Axiom* was singing in a loud, joyful voice!

WALL•E and EVE listened to the words carefully. Confused, they looked at each other. Rudolph? A glowing nose? They thought that Rudolph must be a kind of robot, like WALL•E and EVE. But neither of them had heard of a reindeer-bot before!

WALL•E and EVE sneaked closer to where the humans were working. They called their bot friends over to take a look.

While the robots watched curiously, the humans hung a green circle with small red dots on a storefront. More of the humans started singing. One little girl even shook a silver bell.

Some of the robots had seen behavior like this before, when they were living on the *Axiom*. It seemed to happen every twelve months. They had never been able to figure it out.

WALL•E looked closely at the humans. He tried to understand what made this so different. Then he put his little metal finger on it. The humans looked happy! Most of the time on the *Axiom* they had looked tired and bored. But there was something about what they were doing right then, there on Earth, that seemed to make them very happy.

WALL•E thought that if it made the humans so happy, maybe it would make the robots happy, too!

The robots studied the humans for hours. They stored what they saw in their computer brains. Then they set out to copy the humans. Some of the bots picked up trash left by the humans: bits of tinsel, fake holly, and scraps of brightly colored paper.

The light-bots collected hundreds of strings of lights. WALL•E already had a couple in his trailer. He'd always thought they were pretty, and EVE loved them.

When the electricity was turned on, the lights shone so brightly that they looked like a supernova.

M-O hung up old socks on a wall. He had no idea why anyone would want to put socks on the wall. But the humans were doing it, so he figured that he would, too.

Vacuum-bot sucked up enough packing peanuts to fill several boxes. Unfortunately, he also vacuumed up a nose-full of dust. "Ahhh-chOOOO!" he sneezed. Little white peanuts floated down from the air, coating the floor like a blanket of snow.

WALL•E and EVE roamed the grounds outside the trailer for more things to use. WALL•E went one way. EVE went the other.

EVE picked up a piece of shiny metal. She found some scraps of wrapping paper. She stored them inside her chest cavity. Suddenly, she overheard two humans talking excitedly. One of them was the Captain.

"I just love Christmas, don't you?" the other human said. "The lights, the decorations, the cookies, the presents. Christmas is my favorite time of year!"

Christmas! What a lovely word! EVE rolled it around in her mind. It sparked all her circuits. Was that the name for what the humans were doing?

She stopped to listen more closely to what they were saying.

"Yes," the Captain said slowly. "But don't forget, Christmas isn't about things. That's just what Buy-n-Large wants us to believe. It's about *giving*, not just presents. It's about showing your friends and family that you care about them."

The Captain's words hummed inside EVE. Robots didn't have family, but they did have friends. And she had one friend who meant more to her than any other—WALL•E. He had come to save her when she was on the *Axiom*. He had given her his spare parts. He had cared for her and watched over her. EVE needed to show WALL•E that she appreciated him.

But what kind of present would do that?

EVE roamed far and wide. She searched and searched. She found many pieces of junk, but none of them was quite right. Then, far from WALL•E's trailer, her gaze locked on something small in the dirt. It was the perfect present!

Two days later, it was Christmas Eve. The bots had prepared a celebration just like the humans'. Some of the smaller bots were stirring with excitement. The umbrella-bot wore a pointy red hat with a white pom-pom on top. The robots beeped out the words to the songs they had heard. They didn't always understand the human words, so they made up some on their own.

While all the bots were celebrating the holiday in their own high-tech way, EVE pulled WALL•E aside. She held out a present wrapped in pretty patterned paper.

WALL•E looked surprised. "Ee-vah?" he asked.

EVE nodded. WALL•E turned the present this way and that. He was so busy admiring how the shiny paper shimmered in the colored lights that he almost missed EVE motioning to him.

Open it, EVE signaled.

WALL•E carefully unwrapped the present. He folded up each scrap of paper and laid it on the ground next to him. Finally, he pulled away the last piece.

In his hands, WALL•E held a little evergreen, a miniature Christmas tree.

The longer version of EVE's name was Extra-terrestrial Vegetation Evaluator. She had been trained to find plants and was drawn to the little tree.

She knew that WALL•E, with his kind ways and big heart, would take better care of this present than anyone.

WALL•E and EVE went outside. Together they dug a hole in the earth and planted the Christmas tree. WALL•E gently placed a shiny silver star on top.

WALL•E and EVE looked at the tree. The star twinkled
brightly. It reflected the light from the real stars shining far above
in the night sky.

EVE reached out her hand. WALL•E took it. "Ee-vah," he said.
Now he understood why humans liked Christmas so much.

Disney
Peter Pan
Christmas in Never Land

Wendy sighed as she looked around the Lost Boys' hideout. "Never Land is wonderful," she said, "but it's almost Christmas back home. I do wish we weren't missing it."

"Christmas?" Peter asked. "What's a Christmas?"

"Why, Christmas is the most special time of the year," Wendy said. "There's always a beautiful tree covered with lights."

"And lots of presents!" Michael chimed in.

"Don't forget the Christmas crackers," John added. "They make such a wonderful *kaboom* when they explode!"

"But most important, Christmas is a time to show people how much you care for them," Wendy finished.

Hearing Wendy talk about Christmas gave Peter an idea. "You know," he said, handing Wendy a basket, "a bunch of shells washed up on the other side of Mermaid Lagoon. If you hurry, you can get some before the waves take them back to sea."

"Goodness!" Wendy exclaimed. "If I leave right now, I can be back before dark."

As soon as Wendy was gone, Peter gathered the Lost Boys around him. "We're going to surprise Wendy!" he announced. "We'll have Christmas, right here in Never Land!"

"But how?" John asked.

Peter grinned. "Follow me!" he said.

Peter and the Lost Boys hurried to the village where their friend Tiger Lily lived.

"We need presents for Christmas," Peter told the princess. "And an extra-special gift for Wendy. Do you have any ideas?"

"I know just the thing," Tiger Lily replied.

While Tiger Lily helped Peter make a beautiful beaded necklace for Wendy, her father taught the Lost Boys how to make arrowheads. Everyone had fun making their gifts!

Peter and the Lost Boys thanked Tiger Lily and her father. Then they rushed off to keep preparing their Christmas surprise.

The boys took the gifts back to their hideout. Then they set off on a raid of the *Jolly Roger*.

"Peter, why are we here?" John asked as they hid in the pirate ship's sails. "Surely these savage buccaneers know nothing about Christmas."

"That's true—but they know an awful lot about making things explode," Peter said. "I'm going to swipe some powder from their cannons to make our Christmas crackers!"

Captain Hook was so busy watching for the Crocodile that he didn't notice Peter duck into the *Jolly Roger*'s storeroom. Moments later, Peter burst onto the deck, carrying a bulging bag of powder. He tossed a handful right into Captain Hook's face, making the pirate sneeze.

"Thanks for the powder, you codfish!" Peter Pan shouted.

"I'll get you for this, Pan!" Captain Hook yelled as the boys raced away, laughing.

Next, Peter and the Lost Boys scouted the forest for the perfect Christmas tree. But when they got the tree back to their hideout, Peter frowned. "This tree doesn't look so special," he said.

"That's just because it doesn't have any decorations yet," John assured him.

The Lost Boys went to work. Soon every branch of the tree was decorated with buttons and acorns, arrowheads and seashells, and long garlands of flowers.

In no time, the Lost Boys transformed the hideout. Beneath the festive tree stood piles of presents and stacks of homemade Christmas crackers. But something was still missing.

"The lights!" Peter exclaimed. "Where are the lights?"

"We may have to do without them—" John began. But before he could finish, a clever grin flashed across Peter's face.

"I'll find a way to make our tree light up," he vowed, "or my name isn't Peter Pan!"

Tinker Bell started jingling, but Peter interrupted her.

"No time for chitchat, Tink," he said. "Let's go!"

Peter Pan and Tinker Bell flew through the sky, racing the setting sun all the way to Mermaid Lagoon. The mermaids waved at them from the glittering water.

"Peter!" they cried. "Come tell us one of your stories!"

But Peter didn't have time for stories. Wendy would be home soon, and the Christmas tree still needed lights.

The mermaids shook their heads. "I don't think we can help with that," one said when Peter explained what he needed.

"Why not?" Peter asked. "I've seen the way Mermaid Lagoon lights up at night. If you let me borrow your lights, I'll bring them back tomorrow."

"Mermaid Lagoon lights up because our fish glow in the dark," another mermaid explained as a fish swam by. "The fish won't glow if they leave the water."

By the time Peter and Tinker Bell got home, twilight had fallen.

"There's got to be some way to light that tree," Peter said.

Tink put her hands on her hips and jingled at him. But Peter wasn't listening.

"Not now, Tink. I'm trying to think," he said.

Tinker Bell stormed into her lantern, sending flashes of light around the clearing. That gave Peter a new idea. He hollered for the Lost Boys.

"Fireflies!" Peter announced. "We'll use fireflies to light our Christmas tree!"

The Lost Boys leapt into the air, catching fireflies in their hats. But when they took the fireflies over to the Christmas tree, the glowing bugs flew away.

Peter sat down on an old stump. "It's no use," he said, defeated. "Christmas is ruined."

"Now, now. It's still a very nice tree," John said. "Even if it is getting too dark to see it properly."

Tinker Bell peeked out of her lantern. Maybe *now* Peter would listen to her. She marched right up to him and started jingling and jangling as loudly as she could.

Peter Pan's eyes grew wide. "You mean *you* can make the tree light up?" he exclaimed. "Why didn't you say so before?"

Moments later, Wendy returned to an unusually dark hideout. "Hello?" she called. "Where *is* everyone?"

Suddenly, a lovely glow filled the room as the Christmas tree began to sparkle with pixie dust. Wendy gasped as Peter Pan and the Lost Boys burst out of their hiding places. "Merry Christmas, Wendy!" they cheered.

Wendy beamed and gathered the Lost Boys around her. Christmas had come to Never Land after all.

Disney

ALICE in WONDERLAND

A Present for the Queen

"It looks like Christmas!" Alice said, gazing out her parlor window one cold December afternoon. Snow sparkled in the fields and on the branches of the pine trees. Outside, children were building a snowman. Alice thought about joining them, but the parlor was so warm and cozy.

Alice yawned. Perhaps it would be best to stay inside after all.

Suddenly, something hopped across the snow in front of Alice's house. It was a rabbit with white fur wearing a red coat.

Alice sat up, startled. "Why, it's the White Rabbit from Wonderland!" she cried.

"It's lost! It's lost!" the White Rabbit wailed as he hurried past the house.

Alice quickly put on her winter coat and ran outside after the rabbit. She caught up to him just as he was about to dive into a hole under a tree. "Not so fast!" Alice said. "You're always running away. Whatever is wrong this time?"

"Oh, you must let me through," the White Rabbit cried. "I've lost the Queen of Hearts' Christmas present. If I can't find it, she'll have my head!"

"Oh, dear! That would be awful, indeed," Alice said. "Please let me help you find it!"

But the White Rabbit simply dove down the hole without saying another word.

Alice followed the White Rabbit. Down and down and down she fell until she landed with a thump.

Alice saw the rabbit's fluffy tail disappear through a door. She hurried after him and found herself on a snowy path lined with evergreen trees. The White Rabbit was gone, but Alice could see his footprints in the snow.

Alice made her way down the path, admiring the lights on the trees. Then she noticed something.

"Why, they're fireflies!" she exclaimed.

All at once, the footprints stopped.

"I've lost him again," Alice said with a sigh.

"Lost who?" someone asked.

A toothy smile appeared in one of the trees, followed quickly by a purple striped cat around the smile.

"Cheshire Cat!" Alice cried happily. "Maybe you can help me. The White Rabbit has lost the Queen's present, and—"

"But that's a lost What," the cat interrupted. "I thought you said you lost a Who."

Alice frowned. Usually she quite enjoyed riddles, but she always had such trouble explaining herself to the Cheshire Cat.

"I didn't lose a What," she said. "The White Rabbit did. And now *I've* lost *him*."

Suddenly, the Cheshire Cat disappeared. "I can't help you with your lost Who," he called out, "but I *can* help you with your lost What. Try the Mad Hatter."

Alice looked around. She knew the hatter wasn't on the path behind her, so she continued forward. Soon she heard music.

"Deck the halls with bowls of jelly! Foo loo loo loo loo, loo loo loo loo!"

Alice emerged in a clearing. The Mad Hatter and the March Hare stood with their arms around each other, singing. They stopped when they saw Alice.

"Alice!" the Mad Hatter cried. "Come join us! We're singing Christmas Harolds!"

"Christmas *Harolds*?" Alice asked, confused. "Don't you mean Christmas *carols*?"

"What does Carol have to do with it?" the March Hare said. "Everyone knows Harold wrote all the best Christmas songs!"

And with that, the March Hare and the Mad Hatter began to sing again.

"Oh, Christmas tea, oh, Christmas tea, with milk and cream we drink thee!"

"But that's not how the song goes at all!" Alice said. "And anyway, I don't have time to sing. The White Rabbit has lost the Queen's Christmas present and—"

Suddenly, the Mad Hatter jumped in front of Alice, holding a teapot and a teacup.

"Cold cocoa?" he offered, handing Alice the teacup.

"Don't you mean *hot* cocoa?" Alice replied.

"This reminds me of a riddle," the Mad Hatter said. "What keeps your head cool in the summer and warm in the winter?"

"A hat, of course," Alice said. "Now, please, I need your help. The Queen's present is lost!"

With a twinkle in his eye, the Mad Hatter took off his hat. Sitting atop his head was a large box wrapped in Christmas paper. And lying on top of the box was the tiny, sleepy Dormouse.

"There you are," the Mad Hatter said, grabbing the Dormouse.

"And here *you* are," the March Hare said, handing Alice the present.

"Oh, thank you!" Alice cried. "Now, if you would be so kind—"

But the Mad Hatter and the March Hare weren't listening to her anymore. They had burst into song again.

"On the first day of Christmas, my best friend gave to me, a steaming pot of lovely tea!"

Shaking her head, Alice left the clearing. As she made her way through the trees, she saw that the White Rabbit's footprints had reappeared! Alice didn't want to lose the tracks again.

She carefully followed them . . . all the way to the Queen's castle. As she approached the gates, the Queen's guards grabbed her.

"The Queen's got a reward out for your head!" one of the guards said.

WANTED
ALICE

The guards brought Alice to the throne room, where the White Rabbit was busy apologizing to the Queen.

"I-I'm sorry, Your Majesty," he said. "I had your present, and then I lost it."

The Queen had heard enough. "Off with his head!" she shouted.

"No!" Alice cried, breaking away from the guards. "The present isn't lost. I found it!"

The Queen glared at Alice. "Off with *her* head!" she yelled.

The King coughed quietly and placed his hand on the Queen's arm. "Perhaps you should open the present first, dear," he suggested meekly.

The Queen eyed the present. "I suppose I *could*," she said, tearing off the box's wrapping. Her eyes lit up as she pulled a small Christmas tree out of the box.

As the Queen of Hearts admired her Christmas gift, a large grin appeared in the air next to Alice.

"Now might not be the worst time to slip away," it said.

Alice nodded and quietly snuck out of the room. As soon as she was safely out of sight, she began to run. But she slipped on a patch of ice and hit her head. Everything went black.

When Alice opened her eyes, she found herself back in her parlor. She yawned sleepily.

"What a strange dream I've just had," she said.

Stretching, Alice looked out the window. Just then, her eye caught the finished snowman. It was wearing a familiar hat and holding a teacup.

Alice frowned. Perhaps it *hadn't* been a dream after all. . . .

Snow Puppies

On the day before Christmas, the Dalmatian Plantation was a busy place. The Dalmatian puppies were very excited, for this would be their very first Christmas.

Inside, the puppies watched as Nanny put some boxes with bows beneath the tree. "What is she doing?" they asked their parents, Pongo and Perdita.

"Humans give presents at Christmas to show that they care about each other," Perdita explained.

"Let's give our humans a present," Lucky said.

"I know just what to give them!" Rolly shouted, excited. He ran off and fetched his best bone.

"Humans don't chew bones, silly," Lucky explained.

Later that afternoon, the puppies went for a walk. As they trotted down the path to the village, they saw a group of children playing in the snow.

"We could give our humans a ball," Penny said.

"I don't think Roger and Anita play fetch," Lucky answered. "We need a special gift. But what?"

As he watched the children, Lucky had an idea. "I know a great gift we can make for our humans," he shouted. "Follow me!"

Lucky raced home with the others close behind.

When they reached the Dalmatian Plantation, Lucky started digging in the snow. "Watch me, and do what I do," he called to his brothers and sisters.

The puppies watched with curiosity as Lucky rolled a big pile of snow into a large ball.

From the snowball, he dug out a puppy shape with four legs. But just as he removed the last bit of snow from between the snow puppy's paws, *WHUMP*—it collapsed right on top of him!

"I guess my idea doesn't work," Lucky said, shaking snow from his ears.

"Let's make puppies that are sitting instead of standing up," Patch suggested. "Then maybe they won't fall down."

All afternoon, the little Dalmatians dug and rolled and scooped and scraped the snow into little snow puppy shapes. Freckles, Patch, and Penny even found sticks for tails.

"Our puppies need eyes and noses," Rolly said. "Let's use coal." He and the others ran to the shed and brought back shiny black lumps of coal. One by one, they added eyes and noses to their snow puppies.

Lucky looked at his snow puppy and frowned. "These puppies still don't look like us," he said. "There's something else that's missing. But what could it be?"

Suddenly, Lucky noticed a trail of black paw prints leading from the coal shed across the snowy yard. "That's it!" he shouted. "Our snow puppies need spots."

"Rub your paws in the coal dust," Lucky told the others. "Then you can put black spots on the snow puppies."

The puppies all ran into the coal shed. Then they each
bounded over to their snow puppies.

Working busily, the Dalmatians covered their creations with
tons of black spots.

Soon, it was time to go back inside.

After dinner, Nanny read the puppies a magical Christmas story and tucked them into bed. The puppies were so excited that they wiggled and giggled for a long time.

At last they fell asleep. In their dreams, Roger and Anita were looking at their snow puppies. "What a wonderful surprise!" they heard them say.

On Christmas morning, Roger, Anita, and Nanny gave the puppies their gifts. Each one got a ball, a bone, and a warm red sweater. The puppies loved the presents, but they couldn't wait any longer to give their own.

The puppies ran to the door and began to bark.

"What's the matter with these puppies?" Nanny asked Roger and Anita as the dogs pushed and pulled them toward the door.

When they stepped outside, Roger and Anita began to cheer. In their front yard sat 101 beautiful snow puppies with stick tails, charcoal eyes and noses, and—best of all—lots and lots of very black spots!

Nanny laughed so hard she sat down right in the snow. "Why, that's one hundred and one of the best Christmas gifts I've ever gotten," she said, hugging as many puppies as she could hold.

And everyone agreed that it was so.

Christmas in Monstropolis

Mike Wazowski was Monsters, Inc.'s top Laugh Collector. But one day he had other things on his mind besides work.

Mike walked through the busy streets of Monstropolis. "Come on!" he called to his best friend, Sulley. "We can't be late for the Christmas Committee meeting. I'm in charge of getting the whole city ready!"

Mike had big plans. He pictured Monstropolis glowing from top to bottom. And to cap it off, he planned to set up a huge Christmas tree in the center of the city. "We'll have a special tree-lighting ceremony on Christmas Eve," he told his team. "With a camera crew there to broadcast the event live!"

Sulley nervously looked over Mike's plans. "This is going to take a lot of laugh power, Mikey," he said. "I'm not sure . . ."

But Mike was determined. "People will be talking about the great job the Christmas Committee did for years!" he exclaimed.

Before long, teams of monsters had spread across the city, hanging lights and putting up decorations.

"Maybe we can skip some of these lights," Sulley said. "You know, to save energy."

"Skip lights?" Mike asked. "No, we need *more* lights! Smitty! Needleman!" he shouted to two nearby monsters. "Double the lights in the city dump!"

Soon Christmas Eve arrived. All around Monstropolis, lights shone so brightly that passersby had to squint and shield their eyes. In the city center, hundreds of monsters gathered to witness the tree lighting. TV crews set up cameras to capture the event.

"See, Sulley?" Mike said. "The power is just fine. And you were worried. . . ."

Suddenly, all the Christmas lights went out! Mike looked around in alarm. It wasn't just his decorations that had turned off. The power had gone out across the whole city!

"What's going on, Wazowski?" one monster yelled angrily.

"Yeah!" another monster cried. "We want answers!"

"And lights!" someone else bellowed. The crowd began to murmur angrily.

"Don't worry, folks!" Mike shouted above the growing noise. "Just a little hiccup. We'll have this fixed in a jiffy."

Sulley turned to Mike. "The factory is closed for the holidays," he whispered. "Everyone's on vacation. How exactly are we going to generate enough power?"

"We're going to need to get some substitute Laugh Collectors," Mike said. He scanned the crowd for familiar faces. "Okay, let's see. Who looks funny?" His gaze settled on Smitty and Needleman. "Hey, you two!" he called. "Over here!"

Sulley and Mike quickly ushered their new Laugh Collectors to Monsters, Inc. It was up to the four of them to turn the city's power back on!

At the factory, Sulley stopped short. He gazed at the hundreds of doors hanging from the conveyor belt. Without power, Sulley would need to pull them into place himself.

"We've got our work cut out for us," he said, doing some quick calculations. "We'll probably need six cans to power up the city and have enough left over for the tree lighting. And we've got about an hour to pull it off."

Smitty and Needleman looked nervous. "W-w-what can we do, Mr. Wazoswki?" Needleman asked, his voice shaking. "W-w-we don't know any j-j-jokes."

"Don't worry," Mike said. "I got a million of 'em." He quickly scribbled down some jokes and handed them to the monsters. "And remember: it's all in the delivery."

Mike ran through door after door. "What's a monster's favorite Christmas carol?" he asked a girl. "'Jingle Yells'!"

"What do monster elves learn in school?" he yelled. "The alphabat! Which monster plays holiday tricks? Prank-enstein!"

"That's two cans!" Sulley called out as Mike stepped back onto the Laugh Floor.

"That's all?" Mike slumped to the ground. "I'm ruined!" he groaned. "If we don't get enough power, I'll be the laughingstock of Monstropolis!"

Sulley tried to cheer Mike up, but he knew they had a long way to go. Mike raced in and out of rooms. With half an hour left, they had filled only four cans.

In their rooms, Smitty and Needleman were getting nowhere.

"What's red and white and green?" Needleman nervously asked one boy. Smitty answered in a flat voice: "Santa swimming through seaweed."

The two looked up hopefully. The boy had fallen asleep!

"You stink!" Smitty said as he
and Needleman went through
another door.

"*I* stink?" Needleman's voice rose,
waking the girl whose room they had
entered. Needleman gave Smitty a little
push. "You're the one who smells!"

Smitty tried to push Needleman back.
But Needleman stepped out of the way, and Smitty tumbled to
the floor with a thud. The girl howled with laughter.

"I don't know what you just did in there, but it's working!"
Sulley said when the two stepped back onto the Laugh Floor.
"You just filled half a can!"

The new Laugh Collectors headed through another door. Mike and Sulley heard thumps, crashes, and laughter. Curious, they stopped and poked their heads in.

"I'm on a roll!" Needleman cried, jumping up and down. In a flash, Mike tossed a rotten banana to Smitty.

"Or maybe you're on a . . . banana peel!" Smitty said, gulping down a banana and throwing the peel. Needleman stepped on it and slid across the room. The boy laughed so hard he filled an entire can!

"One more to go!" Sulley said. "And we've only got five minutes left!"

"Good thing I saved the best for last," Mike said, hurrying through the nearest door. "What's red and hairy, has eight legs, and guides Santa's sleigh?" he asked a group of cousins. "Rudolph the red-nosed spider!"

The room shook with laughter.

"Six cans!" Sulley called. "Let's hope it's enough. Tree lighting, here we come!"

The four monsters raced through the streets. The lights had come back on in the city, but what about the Christmas tree? Had they collected enough laughs to light that, too?

By the time they reached the city center, monsters stood shoulder to shoulder, waiting for the lighting. Mike crossed his fingers. He knew all eyes were on him. Taking a deep breath, he flipped the switch. But nothing happened!

"Uh, Mike?" Smitty said, holding up the cord to the tree lights. It wasn't plugged in! Needleman quickly pushed the plug into a nearby socket.

The lights flicked on. Everyone gasped in wonder.

"You did it, Mike!" Sulley said.

Mike shook his head. "You mean *we* did it."

Then he pulled Smitty and Needleman up to face the cheering crowd. "Merry Christmas, Monstropolis!" they all shouted.

Disney Winnie the Pooh

Merry Christmas, Winnie the Pooh!

One snowy Christmas Eve, Winnie the Pooh looked up and down, in and out, and all around his house.

"I have a tree, some candles, and lots of decorations," he said to himself, "but *something* seems to be missing."

Suddenly, a soft knocking sounded on Pooh's door. Perhaps whatever Pooh was missing was just outside!

Pooh opened the door. A small snowman stood shaking on his front doorstep.

"H-Hello, P-Pooh," the snowman said through chattering teeth in a shivery, quivery, but oh-so-familiar voice. "I do like Christmas, but I wish my ears wouldn't get so very cold."

Pooh invited the snowman in. After much melting by Pooh's cozy fireplace, the snowman looked less like a snowman and more like Pooh's best friend, Piglet!

"My!" Pooh said, happy to see a friend where there used to be a snowman.

"My!" Piglet said, now warm enough to notice Pooh's glowing Christmas tree. "Are you going to string popcorn to decorate your tree?" he asked.

"I *had* popcorn and string," Pooh admitted, looking at the popcorn crumbs. "But now there's only string."

"That's okay," Piglet said with a laugh. "We can use the string
to wrap the presents you're giving."

At that, something began to tickle the brain of the little bear.

"I forgot to get presents!" Pooh exclaimed.

"Don't worry, Pooh," Piglet said, trying to smile bravely. "It's the thought that counts."

Soon Piglet left for his own home. He had his own Christmas preparations to finish!

Pooh didn't know what to do about the forgotten presents, but
he did know where to find help.

"Hello!" Pooh called, knocking on Christopher Robin's door.

"Come in, Pooh," Christopher Robin said, smiling as he let his
friend inside. "Why do you look so sad on the most wonderful
night of the year?"

In the excitement of seeing Christopher Robin's Christmas decorations, Pooh forgot all about the presents again. "What are those?" he asked, pointing to some stockings that were hanging above the fireplace.

"Those are stockings to hold Christmas presents," Christopher Robin explained to his friend.

Now Pooh was even sadder. He had just remembered that he didn't have presents—*or* stockings.

Luckily, the bear of little brains was smart enough to have a good friend. Christopher Robin happily gave Pooh stockings for himself and all his other friends.

Pooh thanked Christopher Robin and hurried off to deliver the stockings. "I will get everyone presents later," Pooh said to himself. "The stockings come first."

With a small note that said FROM POOH, he left stockings for Piglet, Tigger, Rabbit, Eeyore, Gopher, Kanga, Roo, and Owl.

Later, back in his own comfy house, Pooh tried to think of presents for his friends. But sleepy Pooh's thinking soon turned into dreaming.

The next morning, Pooh was awakened by a big and bouncy
knock at his door. Sleepily, Pooh opened the door.
"Merry Christmas, Pooh!" his friends shouted.

Pooh was about to apologize for not having any presents for his friends when Piglet, Tigger, Rabbit, Gopher, Eeyore, Kanga, Roo, and Owl started *thanking* him.

"No more cold ears with my new stocking cap," Piglet said.

"My stripedy sleeping bag is Tigger-rific!" Tigger exclaimed.

"So is my new carrot cover," Rabbit chimed in.

Gopher thanked Pooh for the rock-collecting bag, and Eeyore swished his toasty tail-warmer with a slight smile.

Owl announced that his wind sock was perfect for figuring out which way the breeze was blowing. And Kanga and Roo loved their new scarves!

"Something awfully nice is going on," Pooh said. "But I'm not sure how it happened."

"It's called Christmas, buddy bear," Tigger replied.

Then everyone gave their presents to Pooh: lots of pots of delicious sweet honey!

Surrounded by his friends and his favorite tasty treat, Pooh had to agree. "Christmas! What a sweet thought, indeed."

Sleeping Beauty

Aurora's Homemade Holiday

One snowy December day, Princess Aurora and Prince Phillip went for a stroll. As they walked, Phillip noticed that the princess was unusually quiet. "Is something the matter?" he asked.

"My aunts and I used to love Christmastime," she said. The three fairies Flora, Fauna, and Merryweather had raised Aurora in secret and she still thought of them as her aunts.

"Let's invite them for the holidays," Phillip said.

"What a splendid idea!" Aurora cried.

The next morning Prince Phillip sent an invitation to Flora, Fauna, and Merryweather. Then he set off on a short trip to attend to some royal duties.

Aurora was sad to see Phillip go, but she tried to look on the bright side. Now her special Christmas preparations would be a surprise for Phillip when he returned!

Soon the good fairies arrived. Princess Aurora had a special request for them.

"You want a Christmas *exactly* like the ones we shared at the cottage?" Flora asked. "That means we can't use magic."

"You'd better take our wands so we're not tempted to use them," Fauna said to Aurora.

But the wands were hard to catch and zoomed around the room. They did not like the idea of being put away!

"Shall we decorate?" Aurora asked. She led the fairies to baskets of evergreen garland, ornaments, and bows.

"Let's start trimming the tree!" Merryweather exclaimed.

"We should hang the evergreen garland first," Flora said.

Aurora knew that waiting for her aunts to agree on something could take all day. So she suggested that she and Flora put up the evergreen garland while Fauna and Merryweather decorated the Christmas tree.

After a busy morning, the last stocking was finally hung above the fireplace. Then Aurora and the fairies moved on to the kitchen. It was time to begin baking their Christmas treats.

"I can't wait until Phillip tastes your special layer cake," Aurora said, "and the Christmas rolls with jam inside."

"We'll need lots of red frosting," Flora announced.

"Green frosting is prettier," Merryweather argued.

"We'll use both!" Aurora declared.

The next morning over breakfast, Aurora and the good fairies
talked about a gift for Phillip.

"I want to give him a homemade present," Aurora said to her
aunts, "but what?"

"How about a shirt?" Flora suggested.

"But I don't know how to sew," the princess replied.

"We'll show you how," Merryweather said.

Aurora smiled. "Do you remember the stockings you sewed when I was a little girl?" she asked.

"Of course!" Flora said. "We forgot to stitch up the bottoms, and the gifts fell out!"

"You'd say, 'Look, her stocking is empty! We'd better fill it up with more treats!'" Aurora said, chuckling as she remembered the happy times she had shared with the fairies.

All morning, the fairies worked with Aurora, teaching her how to cut fabric and how to sew a shirt.

"Oh, dear," the princess said when she looked down at her sewing. "This shirt isn't looking quite right."

The fairies quickly set aside their own projects to help Aurora with Phillip's shirt.

When Aurora finished Phillip's gift, the fairies helped her get ready. The prince would be home soon.

The fairies made a crown of holly for the princess's hair. Next they had to decide what she should wear. Flora suggested a red dress. Merryweather preferred a blue one. Then Fauna held up a beautiful purple gown. Aurora tried it on. The dress was perfect! Even Flora and Merryweather had to admit the purple dress looked lovely on the princess.

The last thing Aurora had to do was wrap the prince's gift.
Once again, she asked for the fairies' help. When they were
finished, the princess placed the present under the tree.

That afternoon, Prince Phillip arrived back at the castle. Aurora was eagerly waiting for him.

"Close your eyes," the princess said with a sly grin, "and don't open them until I tell you to."

Aurora led Phillip into the grand hall, where the Flora, Fauna, and Merryweather were waiting.

"Okay . . . now open your eyes!" Aurora exclaimed.

Phillip looked around. Crooked wreaths dangled from the walls. The Christmas tree was decorated only on one side. Lopsided cakes, burnt tarts, and misshapen cookies filled a table.

"I've never seen preparations like these before," Phillip said politely. "I can understand why you find them so . . . special."

"Try a lemon tart," Aurora said, holding out a plate.

Phillip took one and bit into it. Suddenly, a strange look came over his face The lemon tart tasted horrible!

"Oh, dear," Fauna said, "we must have forgotten the sugar!"

Aurora handed Phillip his gift. "One more surprise!" she said.

"A shirt!" the prince exclaimed, after opening the box.

But when Phillip tried on his present, the princess and the fairies burst into laughter.

"Oh, dear, that's certainly not the right size," Aurora said. The sleeves were too far too long!

Aurora knew her Christmas wasn't perfect, but sharing a homemade holiday with Phillip and her aunts had made it the best one Aurora could remember!

Christmas Traditions

Lady was excited. It was almost time for Christmas.

"I can't wait to teach the puppies all about our Christmas traditions," she told Tramp one evening.

"Teach them?" Tramp asked. "What is there to teach? Doesn't Christmas just show up one morning?"

"Well, yes," Lady admitted. "But Christmas is about more than just one day of the year. It's about all the things we do together—as a family."

This was Lady's first Christmas with the puppies—and with Tramp. "Just wait until you see the tree all lit up," she told him. "It's magical. And then we hang our stockings by the fire. . . ."

Tramp looked confused. "Why would you hang up stockings?" he asked Lady.

"For Santa Claus to fill with presents, of course," Lady replied.

Just then, the two heard a voice with a thick Scottish accent. "Aye, lad, old Saint Nick will fill your stocking with toys and bones and fancy collars," said their friend Jock, who had joined them.

"My favorite part of the season is the caroling," Trusty added, joining the group. "Miss Lady is a mighty fine singer, and I've been known to howl along pretty well myself."

"I like the lights," Jock said. "It's like having a wee bit of the night sky inside your house."

Lady smiled. "My favorite part is Christmas dinner. We all sit together and eat the most wonderful meal of the year."

"It sounds like quite the celebration, Pidge," Tramp said.

"What's your favorite tradition, lad?" Jock asked.

"I never really celebrated Christmas," Tramp told them. "On the streets, it was just another day. Although the scraps *were* much better than usual."

"Well, all that has changed now," Lady said. "I just know you'll love our holiday traditions, and the puppies will, too. It really is the most wonderful time of the year."

"What's the most wonderful time of the year, Mama?"
Scamp asked, bounding over to his parents.

His siblings—Fluffy, Ruffy, and Scooter—ran after him.
"Mama, Mama," they called. "Jim Dear is bringing a tree *inside*!
What's he doing that for?"

"Christmas, my darlings," Lady answered with a smile.

Lady was right. Christmas *was* magical. The whole house sparkled and shone with decorations and light. The puppies had a great time hanging ornaments on the tree, although Tramp had to help them reach the branches! And Darling even let them sample some of her sweet-smelling Christmas cookies.

One chilly night, the whole family bundled up and went
caroling with Jock and Trusty. Lady *did* have a lovely voice, though
it was hard to hear her over Trusty's howling!

On Christmas Eve, Jim Dear and Darling took the family ice-skating. Fluffy, Ruffy, and Scooter were great skaters, just like their mother. But Tramp and Scamp weren't quite as graceful. They both fell face-first on the ice!

"*This* certainly isn't going to be my favorite Christmas tradition," Tramp said with a laugh as Lady helped him up.

Before bed that night, Lady and Tramp helped the four
puppies hang their stockings by the fire.

"What are these for?" Scamp asked his mother.

Lady smiled. "Just wait and see," she said.

The next morning, the pups awoke to find their stockings stuffed. Santa Claus had come! He had brought a teddy bear for Fluffy, a brush for Ruffy, a squeaky mouse for Scooter, and a big ball for Scamp. Lady got a shiny new water dish, and Tramp got a new bone to chew.

"Merry Christmas, everyone!" Lady said, looking around at her happy family.

Later that evening, Lady was getting the puppies ready when she heard something that made her heart sink.

"Merry Christmas, Aunt Sarah," Jim Dear said as he opened the door. "We're so glad you could come for dinner."

Aunt Sarah greeted Jim and gently set down her Siamese cats, Si and Am. The sly animals crept into the room, sniffed at the puppies, then slowly slipped into the dining room.

Lady turned to Tramp. "We should keep an eye on those two," she said. "You never know what—"

CRASH!

"Oh, no!" Lady cried as they rushed into the dining room. The cats had knocked over the dishes and scattered food everywhere! "Christmas dinner is ruined," she said sadly.

But the cats were not as sneaky as they thought. Darling had seen everything and knew they were the cause of the trouble.

Aunt Sarah apologized and locked the cats in their carrier. Then she helped clean up the mess.

When all the broken dishes and ruined food were gone, Lady and Tramp looked at the empty dining room.

"I'm sorry about dinner, Pidge," Tramp said.

"It's my favorite holiday tradition, and now I don't get to share it with you," Lady said sadly. "I was really looking forward to it."

Suddenly, Tramp had an idea. "Come on," he said. "Let's get Jim Dear, Darling, Aunt Sarah, and the kids. I just realized: I do have my own Christmas tradition to share with you after all."

Tramp led the whole family downtown—to Tony's!

"Eh, Butch!" Tony cried when he saw them walk in. "Welcome to Christmas dinner! We were wondering if we would see you this year. And with such a beautiful family! Come on in!"

"This is perfect," Lady told Tramp as they all sat down to a delicious Italian Christmas dinner.

"Merry Christmas," Tramp said. "May all of our traditions continue for many years—except maybe for ice-skating!"

Mater Saves Christmas

The morning sun sparkled on the snow in Radiator Springs. Mater the tow truck rushed through town carrying a letter for Santa Car. He was just about to mail his letter when he heard a familiar voice behind him.

"Come on, Mater, surely even you know that Santa Car isn't real." It was Lightning McQueen's racing rival, Chick Hicks.

Mater laughed and dropped his letter into the mailbox. "Next you're gonna tell me that the Easter Buggy doesn't exist, either!"

"What are you doing here, Chick?" Lightning asked, looking at his racing rival suspiciously.

"Oh, hey, Lightning, I didn't see ya there. I just came by to donate to Red's toy drive," Chick replied.

Lightning frowned. He had a feeling that Chick was up to no good.

Just then, Sheriff drove up. "I'm afraid I have some bad news, folks. Fill-up stations up and down the route have been robbed. All the gas has been stolen!"

"But without gas, the mail trucks can't deliver our letters to Santa Car!" Mater cried. "That means no Christmas!"

Determined, Mater drove over to the gas pump. "Fill 'er up, Flo," he said. "I'll go to the North Pole and take the letters to Santa Car myself!"

"I'm tryin'," Flo said, "but there's no gas!"

Sure enough, Flo's place had been robbed, too!

Mater narrowed his eyes at Chick, who was standing nearby, chuckling with his friends.

Just then, Fillmore, the hippie van, whispered to Mater, "Meet me at the dome in five."

When Mater got to the dome, he discovered that Fillmore made his own organic fuel. Fillmore filled Mater's tank with the last of his Christmas brew. Then he made Mater promise to put his letter to Santa Car at the top of the pile.

"Never stop believin', man!" Fillmore said.

Back at Flo's, Mater got ready to head out with the letters
for Santa Car. Lightning was worried. He couldn't let Mater go
alone. "Mater, I'm going with you," he said.

"But you don't even have snow tires!" Mater pointed out.

Lightning knew what he had to do. He made a quick pit stop at
Luigi's for new tires. Then Sarge, the army jeep, added some snow
gear of his own—a snowplow, big lights, and fog lamps!

"Now that's what I call good-lookin'! North Pole, here we
come!" Mater exclaimed.

Soon Mater and Lightning started their long journey to the North Pole. The two friends made their way through deep snow. Lightning was tired, but Mater's spirits remained high.

As they trekked on, they sang carols to keep themselves awake. *"Frosty the snowplow—"*

BONK! Suddenly, Mater hit a candy-striped pole.

"The North Pole! We found it!" he cried happily.

"Welcome to the North Pole, gentlemen," Santa Car said.

Lightning stared in amazement. "Santa Car *is* real!" he gasped.

Santa Car was glad that his new friends had carried their letters all that way, but he had some bad news. "Christmas may be canceled this year."

"No Christmas?" Mater cried.

"The reindeer snowmobiles that fly me around the world have been stolen," Santa Car said. "They are fed a top-secret fuel that helps them fly."

Just then, Mater remembered Chick and his friends acting suspiciously at Flo's. "Chick Hicks took your reindeer!" he cried.

"Of course!" Lightning exclaimed. "He wants their fuel! Chick will do anything to win a race."

"I'd tow you to Radiator Springs to find yer reindeer, Mr. Santa Car," Mater said, "but we'd never make it back in time to save Christmas!"

Santa Car had a better idea. He filled Mater's tank with the reindeer snowmobiles' special flying fuel.

Back in Radiator Springs, Luigi and Guido scouted the canyons for the fuel thieves. From a cliff, they spotted Chick and his posse making fuel. Santa Car's reindeer snowmobiles were there, too!

All of a sudden, two of Chick's pals cornered Guido and Luigi.

"You're too late, boys!" Chick shouted at Guido and Luigi. "We've already reverse engineered the flying fuel. I'll fly around the track and never lose to Lightning McQueen again! And you know the best part? No more Christmas! No more dirty oil filters in my stocking! If I can't have presents, no one can!"

Suddenly, the air filled with the sound of jingling bells. Mater
flew over the hill, towing Lightning and Santa Car behind him.

Chick raced away, but Lightning was close behind. Santa Car had filled his tank with the magic fuel, too!

Chick was flying fast, but he was no match for Lightning. As Chick hit a sharp curve, he turned too late, and spun out of control. He tumbled over the edge of a cliff into a cactus patch!

Doc and Mater joined Lightning on the edge of the cliff to take a look at the wreckage.

"Have fun fishin', Mater," Doc said. "Tow him straight to jail!"

Back in town, Mater, Lightning, and the rest of the Radiator Springs gang celebrated the capture of the fuel thieves with Santa Car and his reindeer snowmobiles.

"Well, we better hit the road," Santa Car said. "But you know, we could use some help delivering these presents. What do you say, Mater? Will you help?"

Mater's eyes lit up. "Sure thing!" he yelled. "Let's get 'er done!"

As Mater and Santa Car soared into the sky, Mater looked down at his friends in Radiator Springs and shouted, "Merry Christmas *tow* all, and *tow* all a good night!"

Disney Pinocchio

A Meowy Christmas

"Look, Father—it's snowing!" Pinocchio exclaimed. The little boy gazed out the window at the twinkling village, now covered in a blanket of snow. This was his first winter as a *real* boy. So far he loved everything about it!

"I guess that means it's time we got ready for Christmas," Geppetto told Pinocchio. Figaro, the kitten, wove between them, purring. He was so excited about Christmas!

The next day, Geppetto and Pinocchio went out and bought a Christmas tree. Then they started to decorate.

Geppetto placed his Christmas trinkets around the workshop. Pinocchio hung bows and strands of garland on the walls.

Soon the workshop was filled with holiday cheer.

"It's time for Christmas, Cleo!" Pinocchio told the pretty goldfish, who leaped in excitement while Figaro pranced about the room, playing with the decorations.

That evening, Geppetto and Pinocchio hung stockings on the mantel. Figaro jumped at their feet. He wanted to help, too, but he couldn't reach.

"Great job, Pinocchio!" Geppetto said. As he stepped back to admire their handiwork, he nearly tripped over the active kitten. "Figaro, be careful," Geppetto cautioned.

Figaro hung his head. He had just been trying to help!

Finally, it was time to decorate the Christmas tree.

"Wow, Father!" Pinocchio said. "It sure looks pretty."

"All that's left is to put the star on the top," Geppetto replied. "Pinocchio, you do the honors."

Figaro frowned. He had wanted to put the star on top of the Christmas tree.

With the workshop decorated, Geppetto set about making Christmas Eve supper. He wanted to share all his favorite treats with his new son: stuffing, potatoes, cranberry sauce. . . .

Soon the aromas of herbs and spices and Christmas cookies filled the air.

"Ohhhh, it smells good in here," Pinocchio said, carefully mixing the potatoes.

"Yes! And now it's time for the—Figaro!" Geppetto scolded the kitty, who was about to take a bite of the Christmas goose. "It is not time to eat just yet!"

Feeling hurt and left out, Figaro crept to the bedroom. He would spend Christmas where no one could find him: under Geppetto's bed.

But as he trotted to his hiding place, he noticed something awful. Under the bed was a large pile of presents, and not one was for him!

TO CLEO

TO Pinocchio

TO Geppetto

Just then, the kitten heard Geppetto call, "Figaro, Cleo—we'll be back soon. Be good and don't eat the food while we're gone!"

First Geppetto hadn't gotten him any presents, and now he and Pinocchio were off to have a Christmas adventure without him? That was the last straw. If Figaro couldn't enjoy Christmas, he didn't want anyone else to, either!

When the door closed, Figaro clawed the wrapping
paper on the presents to pieces. He sped around the
workshop, batting at the decorations. He even leaped
at the Christmas tree, knocking all of Pinocchio's
carefully hung ornaments to the ground.

Cleo gurgled at him to stop, but Figaro wouldn't
listen.

Just as Figaro was about to sink his teeth into the Christmas goose, he heard the sound of someone small clearing his throat. It was Jiminy Cricket.

"Now listen here, Figaro," Jiminy said. "The Blue Fairy is none too pleased by your behavior. And who knows what Santa thinks? How will Geppetto and Pinocchio feel when they come back and see what a mess you've made? Is this what Christmas is all about?"

Figaro looked down, ashamed. He knew Jiminy was right.

"Luckily, it's not too late to make things right," Jiminy continued. "And I'm going to help you."

Figaro licked Jiminy's face gratefully and the two got to work repairing all the damage the kitty had done.

They rewrapped the presents and spruced up the tree. They also redecorated the room.

Figaro even added his own holiday decorations. Soon the place sparkled and twinkled brightly, looking as holly and jolly as a Christmas card.

"Not too shabby!" Jiminy observed with an approving nod while Cleo did a happy twirl.

When Geppetto and Pinocchio returned from their outing, they were amazed.

"Wow, Figaro!" Pinocchio cried. "This place looks wonderful!"

Geppetto agreed. "In fact, I'd say you've earned your Christmas present early." And with that, he showed Figaro what he and Pinocchio had gone out to get. "Fresh cream!"

Figaro was overjoyed. Pinocchio and Geppetto hadn't forgotten him after all!

Later that evening, as they all gathered around the table
for their Christmas Eve supper, Figaro sighed happily. He had
learned his lesson. Christmas wasn't about gifts or being the one
to hang the decorations. It was about spending time with family.
And there was nowhere else he'd rather be.

A Perfect Party

Cinderella and her prince sat before a roaring fire. Christmas was coming in a few days, and Cinderella was excited.

"Let's throw a party!" she suggested to the Prince.

"What a splendid idea!" he replied. "How can I help?"

Cinderella smiled. "Just leave everything to me," she said.

The next day, the princess began to decorate.

"May we help, Cinderelly?" Jaq and Gus asked.

"Of course!" she replied. "Let's start with the grand staircase."

The mice were tying some bows when a spool of ribbon began to unwind and roll down the banister. Gus hopped aboard. It was just like a sleigh ride—without the sleigh!

When Cinderella and her friends finished the staircase, they moved on to the rest of the castle. Jaq and Gus helped the princess put garland over the windows in the ballroom.

They tied sprigs of holly over the doorways. They even hung stockings by the fireplaces.

Finally, Cinderella and her friends moved to the stone patio where Cinderella planned to hold her party.

"Won't our guests be chilly out here?" the Prince asked.

"I'm sure it will be fine," Cinderella replied. "Besides, what could be more magical than celebrating under the stars?"

"I like stars. They're twinkly," Gus said as he nibbled on a popcorn garland.

"Gus!" Jaq scolded. "You're supposed to be hanging decorations, not eating them!"

Later Cinderella went to the royal sewing room. When Prudence, the head of household staff, peeked in, she saw the princess sewing a handkerchief.

"Why don't you ask the royal seamstresses to do that?" Prudence suggested.

"I'm making presents for our guests," Cinderella said. "It's so much more personal if I do it myself."

On Christmas Eve, the royal chef came to speak with Cinderella.
He wanted to know what he should cook for the party.

"Not a thing," Cinderella replied.

Later Prudence saw her in the storeroom filling baskets with
fruit, ears of corn, and different kinds of cheese. She was appalled.

Back on the patio, Cinderella laid out the food.

"Hmmm," she said. "Something's missing—but what?"

Suddenly, Cinderella's fairy godmother appeared.

"My dear, you need a centerpiece," she said. Waving her magic wand, she turned a water pitcher into an ice sculpture!

"Now everything is perfect for our holiday picnic!" Cinderella exclaimed.

When Cinderella left to change her gown, the Fairy
Godmother slipped into the banquet room. "Oh, no," she said,
looking at the decorations Cinderella and the mice had hung.
"This will never do for a royal ball."

The Fairy Godmother waved her wand. Instantly, an elaborate
feast appeared. She waved her wand twice more, and the court
musicians appeared, ready to play.

"Now, that's more like it," the Fairy Godmother said.

When Cinderella and the Prince walked past the banquet room, the princess couldn't believe her eyes.

Just then, Prudence rushed in. "Where are your guests?" she asked Cinderella.

"My party isn't being held in here," Cinderella told her.

"Then what is?" Prudence asked.

Thinking quickly, the princess said, "A Christmas party in honor of the royal staff. Would you please tell the others?"

"What a wonderful surprise!" the housekeeper exclaimed.

Cinderella opened the patio doors. "Merry Christmas!"

A chorus of chirps, barks, and whinnies answered her. All of Cinderella's animal friends had gathered for her party.

"Happy Christmas, Cinderelly!" Gus shouted.

"Merry Christmas," Jaq said, correcting him.

Cinderella's animal friends loved the meal she had prepared. Afterward, it was time for presents! There were new feed bags, cozy blankets, and stylish mouse-sized outfits. Jaq loved his new jacket so much that he wouldn't stop looking at his reflection.

Later the Prince and Cinderella danced underneath the stars. When they stopped, they realized they were alone.

"Oh, my! Look!" Cinderella cried. Their animal friends had gone inside and were with the staff. Delighted that everyone was getting along, Cinderella and the Prince joined them.

It was the most unusual—and the merriest—Christmas celebration the kingdom had ever seen!